I LOVE MY BROTHER!

Written By

Alana Huizenga

Illustrated By

R.K. Blessing

Book Design & Production: Columbus Publishing Lab • www.ColumbusPublishingLab.com

Paperback ISBN 978-1-63337-114-9 • E-book ISBN 978-1-63337-115-6

Printed in the United States of America
1 3 5 7 9 10 8 6 4 2

This book is dedicated to my favorite little monkeys, Milo and Harper.

Thank you for all the inspiration!

I love my brother all day long...

When it's time to wake up...

When it's time to go to sleep...

and all the hours in between...

I love my brother when he climbs on the sink...

and when he wants to color me pink

I love my brother when he cries in the car...

and when he plays my favorite guitar

I love my brother when he wants to flee...

and when he tries to act like me

I love my brother when he throws his food...

and when he's in a splashy mood

I love my brother when he wants to help me get dressed...

and when it's time to pick out books
but he'd rather make a mess

No matter what I love my brother...

even when he hogs my mother

Don't forget to keep your eyes peeled

CPSIA information can be obtained at www.ICGtesting.com
Printed in the USA
BVOW05s0330260816

460126BV00003B/4/P

9 781633 371149